Stony and Goliath

THE TRUE HERO

EL VERDADERO HÉROE

Piedrín y Goliat

Written by **David P. Alcorta** · Illustrated by **Jill M. Schmidt** · Translated by **Ernesto G. Pino**

BOOK PUBLISHERS NETWORK

Published by
Book Publishers Network
PO Box 2256
Bothell, WA 98041
425 483-3040
www.bookpublishersnetwork.com

ISBN10: 1-887542-72-8
ISBN13: 978-1-887542-72-8
LCCN: 2008922006

Book design: Jill M Schmidt

10 9 8 7 6 5 4 3 2 1

In loving gratitude to

Dora,

the love of my life for sharing her life with me.

Together we dedicate this book to our grandchildren
listed according to age:

Makaylia
Chase
Cole
Rio
Cage
Chile
Tresan

In the beginning God created the sky, water, and land.

The land was filled with many beautiful things: soil, trees, and stones.

As in all of His creations, God took special interest in making stones which He fashioned into different colors and sizes.

palm

La Palmera

Dios en el principio creó el cielo, el agua, y la tierra.

Muchas cosas hermosas llenaron el paisaje: la tierra, los árboles, y las piedras.

Como todo lo creado por Él, Dios puso especial interés al hacer las piedras y las diseñó de diferentes colores y tamaños.

brook

El Arroyito

When Stony was young, he said to Mama and Papa Stone, "I don't like being so small. I want to be big like Boulder, strong like Granite, beautiful like Marble, shiny like Jade, and able to shoot fire like Flint!"

butterfly

La Mariposa

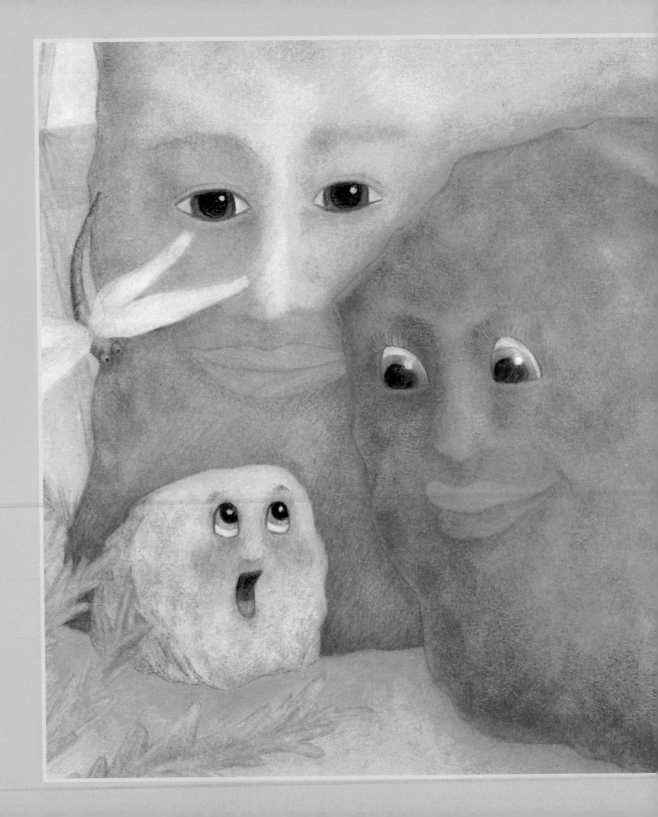

Cuando Piedrín era niño le dijo a Mamá y Papá Piedra: "No me gusta ser tan pequeño. ¡Quiero ser grande como Peñasco, fuerte como Granito, hermoso como Mármol, brillante como Jade y poder disparar fuego como Sílice!"

leaf

La Hoja

Mama Stone said, "You're a beautiful little stone and someday you may mature to be a strong corner stone like Papa Stone."

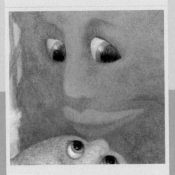

Mother

La Mamá

Mamá Piedra dijo: "Tú eres una hermosa piedrita y algún día puede que madures y seas una piedra principal como Papá Piedra".

Years went by, and Stony played with his friends. He rolled around on the banks of a little babbling brook.

As he played and tumbled around with the bigger stones, Stony developed into a smooth young stone.

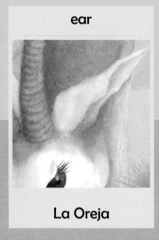

ear

La Oreja

Pasaron los años y Piedrín jugaba con sus amigos. Rodaba por las riveras de un pequeño arroyo.

Mientras jugaba y rodaba con las piedras más grandes, Piedrín se transformó en una piedra joven y lisa.

One day Stony was real sad because Papa Stone was called to be the corner stone for the new village temple.

Stony's friends, Marble and Granite, had been chosen to help build beautiful village buildings and statues.

Jade was polished to make beautiful jewelry, Flint was asked to light fires to keep the homes warm, and Boulder was asked to mark and guard the entrance of the village.

Un día Piedrín se puso muy triste porque a Papá piedra lo llevaron para ser la piedra principal del nuevo templo del pueblo.

A los amigos de Piedrín, Mármol y Granito, los eligieron para ayudar a construir hermosos edificios y estatuas para el pueblo.

A Jade lo pulieron para que fuera una bella joya, a Sílice le pidieron que prendiera los fuegos que mantendrían los hogares cómodos y a Peñasco le pidieron que marcara y vigilara la entrada del pueblo.

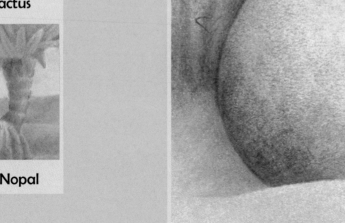

cactus

El Nopal

sheep

Las Ovejas

As Papa Stone was carried off to be the corner stone for the new temple, Stony cried out, "Papa! What about me? No one will know I'm here!"

Papa smiled and said, "Be patient, Stony. God has a special place for you."

flower

La Flor

Cuando llevaban a Papá Piedra para ser la piedra principal del templo nuevo, Piedrín gritó: "¡Papá! ¿qué pasará conmigo? ¡Nadie sabrá que estoy aquí!"

Papá sonrió y dijo: "Ten paciencia, Piedrín. Dios tiene un lugar especial para ti."

village

El Pueblo

As the years went by, the swift water and hot sun turned Stony's body hard and smooth.

He was very good-looking but very small.

horns

Los Cuernos

Los años pasaron y las rápidas aguas y el caliente sol transformaron a Piedrín haciéndolo fuerte y liso.

Era guapísimo pero muy pequeño.

Stony cried, "I am so small; no one will ever use me for anything!

"Why did God make me so small?"

mouse

El Ratón

Piedrín lloró: "¡Soy tan pequeño que nadie me usará para nada!

"¿Por qué Dios me hizo tan pequeño?"

One day while Stony lay on the bank of the babbling brook, he heard someone coming.

It was the shepherd boy, David.

"Oh," said Stony, "I hope he comes closer so that I can see him."

stones

Las Piedritas

Un día mientras Piedrín estaba a la orilla del arroyito, oyó que alguien venía.

Era David, el pastorcito.

"Oh," dijo Piedrín, "Espero que David se acerque para poder Verlo."

David's footsteps got closer and closer and stopped right in front of Stony. David looked young and brave.

The shepherd boy looked straight at Stony.

Stony didn't know what to do, for no human had ever noticed him before.

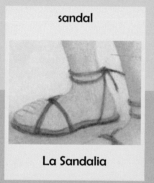

sandal

La Sandalia

Los pasos de David se acercaron más y más y se detuvieron bien frente a Piedrín. David era joven y valiente.

El pastorcito miró directamente a Piedrín.

Piedrín no sabía qué hacer porque jamás se había fijado en él un humano.

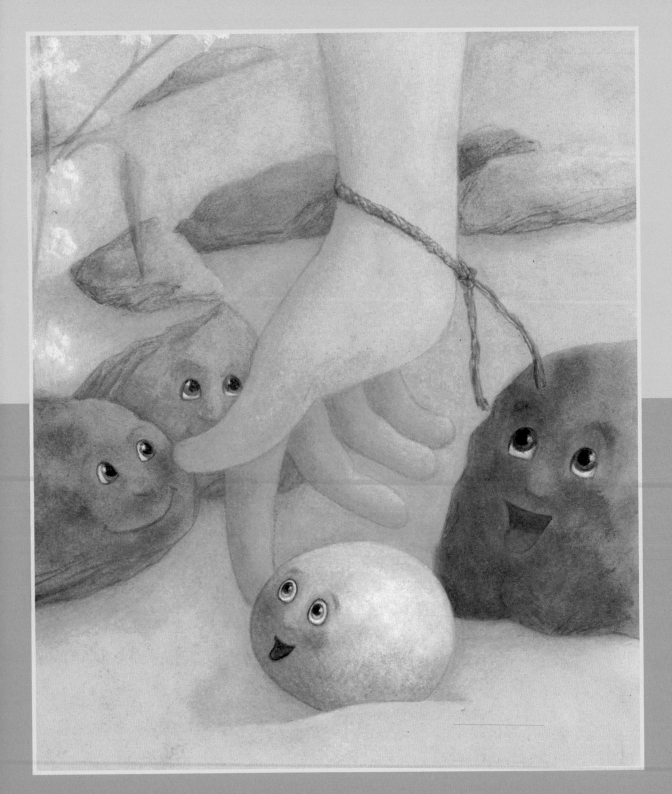

The shepherd boy reached down to Stony.

"Oh my! He is going to pick me up," said Stony, and all the other stones cheered with joy because the shepherd boy had chosen Stony.

hand

La Mano

El pastorcito se agachó y estiró el brazo hacia Piedrín.

"¡Uy! Me va a levantar," dijo Piedrín, y todas las demás piedras gritaron con alegría porque el pastorcito había elegido a Piedrín.

David held Stony in his hand,
smiled and said,

"You are perfect. I have to do a
job for God. Would you like to
help me?"

"Oh yes, yes!" cried Stony.
"I have never been chosen to do
anything!"

Stony was so proud.

face

La Cara

David tomó a Piedrín en su
mano, sonrió y dijo:

"Eres perfecto. Tengo que hacer
un trabajo para Dios. ¿Quieres
ayudarme?"

"¡Oh sí, sí! Gritó Piedrín.
"¡Me escogieron
para hacer algo!"

Piedrín estaba tan orgulloso.

David put Stony into his sling and whirled him around and around. Stony had never felt the wind like this before.

Stony was happy and ready.

soldier

El Soldado

David puso a Piedrín en una
honda y lo hizo dar vueltas y vueltas. Piedrín nunca había
sentido el viento así antes.

Piedrín estaba contento y listo.

sword

La Espada

All of a sudden Stony was released from the sling. He could move quickly through air because he was smooth and strong.

He was on his own out to do a job for God.

He flew straight and true and smashed against the head of Goliath, the big, bad bullying giant.

sling

La Honda

De pronto, Piedrín fue lanzado de la honda. Pudo volar rápidamente por el aire porque era liso y fuerte.

Estaba listo para hacer un trabajo para Dios.

Voló directo y seguro y se chocó con la cabeza de Goliat, el gigante grandote y bravucón.

eye

El Ojo

Stony bounced back onto the ground as the big bad giant fell to his knees and onto his face.

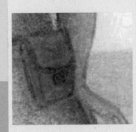

pouch

La Bolsita

Piedrín rebotó en el suelo mientras el gigante malvado caía de rodillas y de frente.

His friends cheered with joy because Stony had been chosen to do a job for God.

lizard

La Lagartija

Los amigos de Piedrín lo alentaban con alegría porque él había sido elegido para hacer un trabajo para Dios.

Mama and Papa Stone celebrated with great joy because God had made Stony perfect.

Stony had become the most special stone of all.

Father

El Papá

Mamá y Papá Piedra festejaron con gran alegría porque Dios hizo a Piedrín perfecto.

Piedrín ahora es la piedra más especial de todas.

Somewhere on the banks of that little babbling brook, Stony is happily rolling around with his friends.

Today he is filled with joy and happiness.

He no longer wants to be like anyone else because he knows that God made him perfect.

smile

La Sonrisa

En algún lugar de las riveras de aquél arroyito, Piedrín está rodando alegremente con sus amigos.

Hoy está lleno de alegría y felicidad.

Ya no quiere ser más como los otros porque sabe que Dios lo hizo perfecto.

Today no one remembers
Stony.

All anyone remembers is the
story about David and Goliath.

cap

La Gorra

Hoy nadie recuerda a Piedrín.

Todo lo que los demás recuerdan es la historia de David y Goliat.

THE END

FIN

Blessings
Deacon
David P. Alcorta
2008

Deacon David P. Alcorta

David P. Alcorta was born in Kerrville, Texas, and moved to the Pacific Northwest in 1965, where he now lives with his wife, Dora, two children, and seven grandchildren. He is now retired from a career in public administration and human services for the local and federal governments. He currently enjoys a full-time ministry as an ordained deacon and volunteers for the American Red Cross and the City Community Emergency Response Team for local and national disasters. David now pours his experiences from human service, spiritual energy, and storytelling into his Sunday sermons and the writing of his first book, ***Stony and Goliath the True Hero***.

Before Nintendo, iPods, Xbox, and even TV, storytelling entertained all ages during the quiet moments of the day. For David, it is a family tradition, handed down through generations of storytellers in his family. David says, "I have been telling stories since I was a little boy. My uncles sat me on their knee and asked me to tell them stories. Everyone laughed at my outrageous imagination. Now I love to tell children's stories because it allows me to be in the presence of my youth."

And coming soon, watch for...

Dani the Dandelion